BRAVE LITTLE TAILOR

by the
Brothers Grimm

Illustrated by
Mark Corcoran

Troll Associates

Troll Associates, Mahwah, N.J.

Library of Congress Catalog Card Number: 78-18075
ISBN 0-89375-137-5

One morning, a little tailor was hard at work in his shop. Suddenly he heard an old woman calling, "Good jelly to sell! Good jelly to sell!" So he bought some jelly, and spread it on his bread. Soon, hungry flies were buzzing around the sweet jelly.

The tailor swung at the flies, and when he counted the dead ones, he saw that there were seven. So he decided to make himself a belt, on which he stitched the words *Seven At One Blow*.

Then he put a piece of cheese in his pocket and went outside. Next, he caught a small bird and put the bird in his pocket next to the cheese. Then he set off toward a distant mountain.

When he reached the top of the mountain, he saw a terrible giant. "Good morning," said the tailor. "I am off to seek my fortune. Would you care to join me?"

But the giant roared, "Hah! Why should I go with a
miserable little rascal like you?"

The tailor showed his belt to the giant: *Seven At One Blow.* The giant thought it meant that the tailor had killed seven *men.* So he decided to put the tailor to a test. First, the giant picked up a rock, and squeezed it until water dripped out. "Can you do that?" he roared.

"Easily!" replied the tailor, taking the cheese from his pocket. He squeezed it until drops of liquid fell to the ground.

"Not bad," said the giant. Then he picked up a stone and threw it high into the sky. "Try to beat that!" he roared.

"I will throw one so high that it never comes down," announced the little tailor. He took the bird from his pocket and tossed it into the air. The bird was so happy to be free that it flew far, far away.

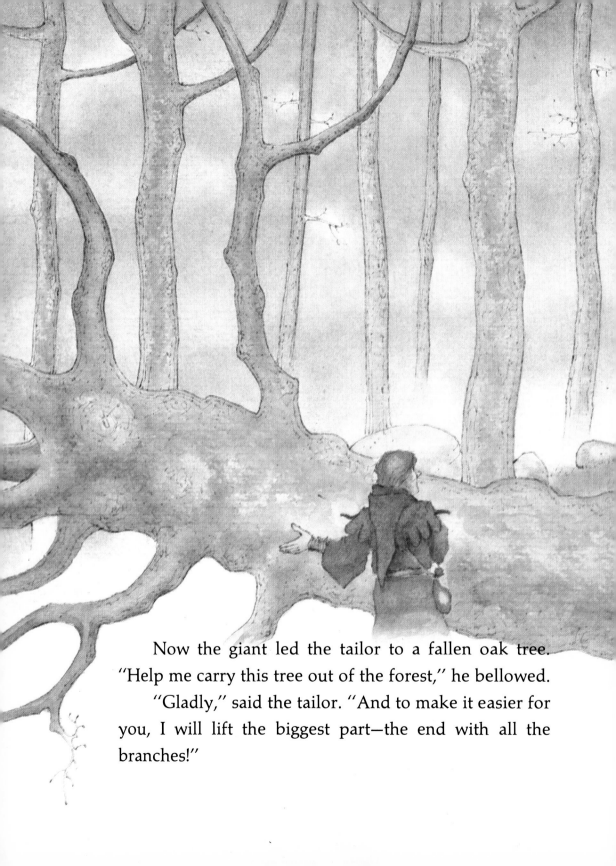

Now the giant led the tailor to a fallen oak tree. "Help me carry this tree out of the forest," he bellowed.

"Gladly," said the tailor. "And to make it easier for you, I will lift the biggest part—the end with all the branches!"

So the giant lifted the heavy trunk of the tree. Behind him, the clever tailor sat down on the branches, instead of carrying them. Soon the giant grew tired. "I can go no farther!" he cried, dropping the tree.

The tailor laughed. "Why, you can't even carry your end of this little tree!"

Soon they came to a cherry tree. The giant bent it
down to the ground, and ate the sweetest fruit from the
highest branch. Then he told the tailor to hold it and pick
some cherries for himself. But when the giant let go, the
tree sprang back, throwing the tailor high into the air.

"Oh ho!" laughed the giant. "You are too weak to hold down a tiny twig!"

"You are mistaken," replied the tailor. "I *jumped* over the tree. That's something *you* can't do!"

And the giant tried, but he landed in the branches.

That night, the giant brought the tailor to his cave, where he lived with some other giants. When he thought the tailor was asleep in his bed, the giant took a heavy iron bar and smashed the bed to pieces. "That's the end of

you!" he grunted. But the tailor was asleep in a corner of
the cave, for the bed had been too big. And in the
morning, when they saw that the tailor was alive and
well, the terrified giants ran from the cave.

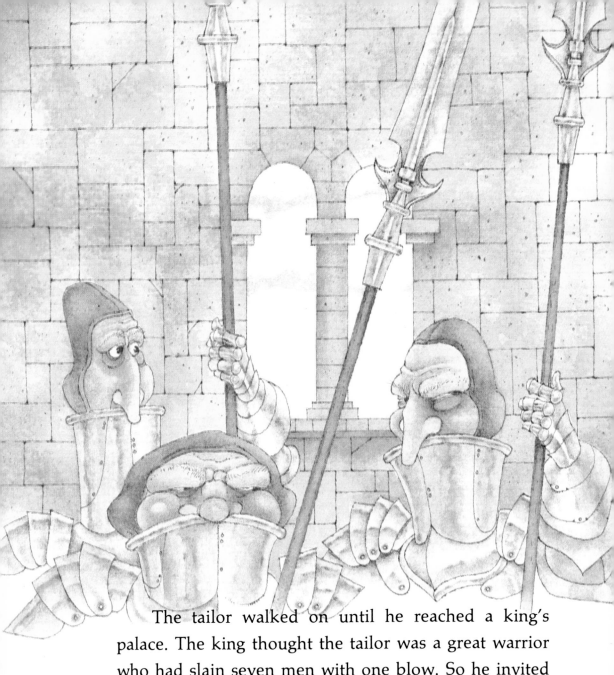

The tailor walked on until he reached a king's palace. The king thought the tailor was a great warrior who had slain seven men with one blow. So he invited the tailor to join his army. But the other soldiers grumbled and complained. They were jealous of the tailor. They told the king that they would not serve in the army with such a mighty warrior. The king had a problem. He did not want all his soldiers to leave, but he was afraid to

send the tailor away. Finally, the king thought of a plan.

He called for the tailor, and said, "In the woods live two terrible giants. If you can slay them, I will give you half my kingdom, and my daughter's hand in marriage."

The tailor agreed, and set off into the forest. Soon he saw the giants, asleep under a tree. He climbed the tree, and began dropping stones on them. One of the giants awoke and asked his friend, "Why are you hitting me?"

"I am not hitting you," replied the second giant. "You are dreaming. Go back to sleep." Then the tailor dropped stones on the second giant, who pushed his friend and roared, "Stop throwing things at me!"

And the first giant replied, "I am throwing nothing!" They argued for a while, but finally fell asleep again.

Then the tailor took the heaviest stone, and heaved it down from the tree. It hit the first giant, who cried, "This is too much!" He gave the other giant such a blow that the earth shook! Then they ripped up trees by the roots and beat each other unmercifully. When it was over, both giants lay dead on the ground.

The king was upset when he saw that the tailor was still alive, for he did not want to keep his promise. "Now you must capture the wild unicorn that lives in the forest," he said.

So the tailor went back into the forest. Before long, the unicorn saw him and came running toward him. At the very last moment, the tailor jumped aside, and the unicorn caught its horn deep in a tree. The tailor cut down the tree, and led the unicorn back to the king.

But the king had yet another task for the brave little
tailor. "There is a wild boar in the woods," he said.
"Capture him, and you will receive your reward."

So once again, the tailor entered the woods. As soon as the wild boar saw him, it began to charge. The tailor ran into a hut, and jumped out the back window. The boar ran into the hut, but was too big to jump out the window. Then the tailor ran around to the front and slammed the door shut, trapping the beast inside.

Now the king had no choice but to keep his promise.
So the brave little tailor married the princess, and re-
ceived half the king's land.

One night, the young bride overheard the tailor talking in his sleep about measuring, cutting, and sewing. So she knew he was only a tailor, and not a great warrior.

In the morning she told her father, who said, "Leave your door open tonight. My soldiers will tie him up, and carry him to a ship that will take him to the ends of the earth."

But the tailor found out about the king's plans. That night, he closed his eyes, but did not sleep. When he heard his bride sneak out of bed and open the door, he pretended to talk in his sleep. "I have killed seven at one blow, slain two giants, taken a unicorn, and captured a wild boar. So why should I be afraid of a few ordinary soldiers who are hiding outside my door?"

When they heard this, the soldiers ran for their lives.
And for the rest of his days, the brave little tailor
remained a king.